# HERMES

*God of Travels and Trade*

BY TERI TEMPLE

ILLUSTRATED BY ROBERT SQUIER

Published by The Child's World®
1980 Lookout Drive • Mankato, MN 56003-1705
800-599-READ • www.childsworld.com

Acknowledgments
The Child's World®: Mary Berendes, Publishing Director
The Design Lab: Design and production
Red Line Editorial: Editorial direction

Design elements: Maksym Dragunov/Dreamstime;
Dreamstime

Photographs ©: Shutterstock Images, 5, 12; iStockphoto,
20, 29; Jose Ignacio Soto/Shutterstock Images, 23

ISBN 9781614732624
LCCN 2012932419

Printed in the United States of America
Mankato, MN
July 2012
PA02119

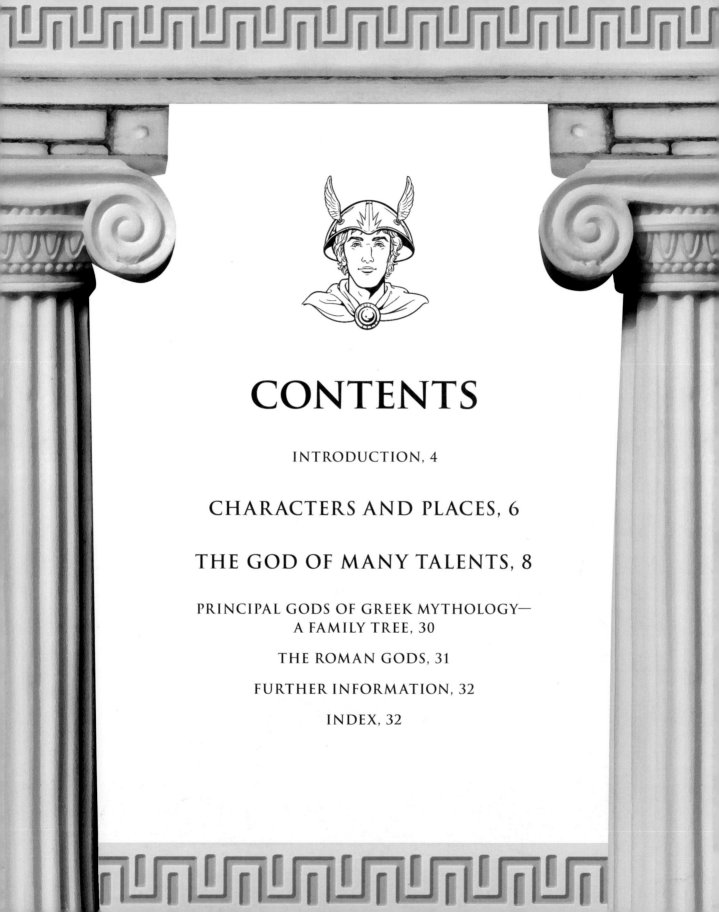

# CONTENTS

# INTRODUCTION

Long ago in ancient Greece and Rome, most people believed that gods and goddesses ruled their world. Storytellers shared the adventures of these gods to help explain all the mysteries in life. The gods were immortal, meaning they lived forever. Their stories were full of love and tragedy, fearsome monsters, brave heroes, and struggles for power. The storytellers wove aspects of Greek customs and beliefs into the tales. Some stories told of the creation of the world and the origins of the gods. Others helped explain natural events such as earthquakes and storms. People believed the tales, which over time became myths.

The ancient Greeks and Romans worshiped the gods by building temples and statues in their honor. They felt the gods would protect and guide them. People passed down the myths through the generations by word of mouth. Later, famous poets such as Homer and Hesiod wrote them down. Today, these myths give us a unique look at what life was like in ancient Greece more than 2,000 years ago.

## ANCIENT GREEK SOCIETIES

IN ANCIENT GREECE, CITIES, TOWNS, AND THEIR SURROUNDING FARMLANDS WERE CALLED CITY-STATES. THESE CITY-STATES EACH HAD THEIR OWN GOVERNMENTS. THEY MADE THEIR OWN LAWS. THE INDIVIDUAL CITY-STATES WERE VERY INDEPENDENT. THEY NEVER JOINED TO BECOME ONE WHOLE NATION. THEY DID, HOWEVER, SHARE A COMMON LANGUAGE, RELIGION, AND CULTURE.

**MOUNT OLYMPUS**
*The mountaintop home of
the 12 Olympic gods*

*Aegean Sea*

# ANCIENT GREECE

**MOUNT CYLLENE**
*Birthplace of Hermes*

**PYLOS, GREECE**
*A town in Greece where Hermes
hid his stolen cattle in a cave*

CRETE

**OLYMPIAN GODS**
*Demeter, Hermes, Hephaestus, Aphrodite, Ares, Hera,
Zeus, Poseidon, Athena, Apollo, Artemis, and Dionysus*

**TITANS**
*The 12 children of Gaea and Cronus; godlike giants
that are said to represent the forces of nature*

**APOLLO** (a-POL-lo)
*God of sun, music, healing, and prophecy; son of Zeus and Leto; twin to Artemis*

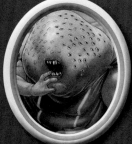

**ARGUS** (AHR-guhs)
*A monster with 100 eyes; Hera's servant*

**AUTOLYCUS** (aw-TOL-i-kuhs):
*Son of Hermes; most famous thief in ancient Greece*

**FATES** (FEYTS)
*The three goddesses of fate, they determine when life begins and ends; daughters of Zeus*

**GRAEAE** (GREE-ee)
*The gray sisters who were guardians of the Gorgons; shared one eye and one tooth among them*

**HERA** (HEER-uh)
*Queen of the gods; married to Zeus*

**HERMES** (HUR-meez)
*Messenger to the gods; god of travel and trade; son of Zeus*

**IO** (EE-oh)
*Companion of Zeus who was changed into a white cow; linked with the Egyptian god Isis*

**MAIA** (may-YUH)
*Eldest daughter of the Titan Atlas; mother of Hermes by Zeus*

**MEDUSA** (muh-DOO-suh)
*A snake-haired creature whose gaze can turn people to stone; mother of Pegasus; killed by Perseus*

**PAN** (PAN)
*God of nature; son of Hermes; has the legs, horns and tail of a goat*

**PERSEUS** (PUR-see-uhs)
*Greek hero who killed Medusa; married to Andromeda*

**ZEUS** (ZOOS)
*Supreme ruler of the heavens and weather and of the gods who lived on Mount Olympus; youngest son of Cronus and Rhea; married to Hera; father of many gods and heroes*

Hermes was the merriest of all the gods on Mount Olympus. He was also clever. This helped him secure a spot as one of the 12 Olympian gods. Hermes's tale is like many of his brothers and sisters. It began with his father Zeus and Zeus's desire for more wives and children. Zeus was the supreme ruler of heaven and the earth. As king of the gods, Zeus also ruled Mount Olympus. At his side was his wife Hera. She was beautiful, but she could be very jealous. She knew Zeus had other wives and children. She just did not like sharing him. So Zeus snuck behind Hera's back to see his other wives and beautiful maidens on Earth.

Hermes's mother was the lovely mountain nymph Maia. She was one of the seven daughters of the Titan Atlas. The sisters were known as the Pleiades. Maia was the oldest sister. She lived in a cave high atop Mount Cyllene in southern Greece. Zeus would slip out while Hera was asleep to visit Maia. The cave was so deep that Hera never saw Maia. Hera did not know that Maia was another wife of Zeus. She also did not know that Maia was pregnant. Maia gave birth to her son Hermes in the cave without Hera knowing. Hermes later tricked Hera into accepting him. Hermes proudly took his spot next to the other gods at the palace on Mount Olympus.

Hermes was a very smart baby who could learn quickly. Even on the day he was born he caused mischief for the gods. Born at dawn, Hermes was ready to explore his world by noon. As his mother slept, he snuck out of the cave. Hermes's first discovery was a tortoise shell. He added strings to the shell and created the first lyre. The lyre was a stringed instrument much like a small harp. Hermes quickly taught himself how to play it. The songs he played were enchanting.

But Hermes was not done for the day. He set off to explore the countryside. He soon came across a whole herd of cattle. His older brother Apollo was supposed to be guarding the cattle. But Apollo was nowhere to be seen. So Hermes decided to steal 50 animals from the herd. Hermes needed a plan to get the animals away from the pasture. He did not want anyone to find the cows, especially Apollo.

Hermes had to cover his tracks. He cleverly tied brooms to the cows' tails. When the cows moved their tails, they swept away their footprints in the dirt. Hermes also tied shrub branches to the cows' feet. To confuse Apollo even more, Hermes led the cows out of the pasture backward so it looked like they had gone in the opposite direction. Hermes felt sure he would get away with his crime. He sacrificed two of the cattle to the Olympic gods. Hermes wanted to thank them for his good fortune. Hermes hid the animals in a cave in the town of Pylos. He then crawled back into bed with his mother and fell asleep.

Apollo later returned to the pasture and found that 50 animals were missing from the herd. He searched all over the world for them. Apollo could not find where they had gone. He had to use his powers of prophecy to find them. A prophecy is a prediction of what is to come.

### THIEVES OF ANCIENT GREECE

SOME OF THE STRICTEST LAWS IN ANCIENT GREECE WERE FOR STEALING. THE WORST KIND OF THIEF WAS ONE THAT STOLE FROM HOUSES AT NIGHT. ANY CITIZEN COULD ACCUSE ANOTHER OF A CRIME. IF CAUGHT IN THE ACT, THE THIEF WAS

Apollo's gift of looking into the future would help him solve the mystery. His visions led him to Hermes. Curled up asleep next to his mother, Hermes looked like an innocent baby. Apollo knew better though.

EXECUTED IMMEDIATELY. IF NOT, THE CASE WENT BEFORE COURT. THE GUILTY THIEF COULD BE FINED, BANISHED, OR WHIPPED AND THEN EXECUTED. THE ANCIENT GREEKS AND ROMANS PLACED WOODEN POSTS WITH THE HEAD OF HERMES CARVED INTO THEM AT THE ENTRANCES OF THEIR HOMES. THESE CRUDE HEADS WITH BEARDS WERE THOUGHT TO PROTECT AGAINST THIEVES.

Apollo accused Hermes of stealing his cattle. But Hermes said he was innocent. Apollo searched the cave and could not find any trace of the cows. Not satisfied, Apollo brought his complaint to their father Zeus. Hermes was clever, but he could not fool his father. Hermes did manage to distract Apollo during the hearing. He then stole Apollo's silver bow and arrows. Zeus was amused by his new son's pranks. Still he insisted that Hermes return the cattle to his big brother.

Hermes agreed and led Zeus and Apollo to the cave on Pylos. Apollo was again furious when he discovered two of the animals missing. Hermes quietly began to play his lyre. Apollo quickly forgot about the missing cattle as he listened to the beautiful music. As the god of music, this unusual instrument was very interesting to Apollo. He wanted to know all about it and how it made such lovely sounds. Apollo decided to trade the entire herd of cattle to Hermes for his lyre.

Hermes then returned Apollo's bow and arrows. Apollo had not even realized they were missing. He was beginning to like his playful little brother. Apollo and Hermes would become great friends over time.

Hermes gained more skills as a thief as he grew older. He stole the girdle of Aphrodite (the goddess of love), the tools of Hephaestus (the god of fire, metalwork, and building), and the trident of Poseidon (the god of the sea). Hermes even thought about taking Zeus's thunderbolt, but he was afraid of getting burned. The gods on Olympus were getting used to Hermes's tricks. So, Hermes became the patron god of thieves, liars, and troublemakers.

Hermes also had a good side. He was often shown as a beardless youth. Humans credited any sort of good luck to Hermes. If they found treasure, it was sure to be a gift from Hermes. Hermes became connected with any gain, honest or otherwise. As a result his titles included god of diplomacy, trade, and commerce.

| Greek Letter | Name | English Equivalent |
|---|---|---|
| A (α) | Alpha | a |
| B (β) | Beta | b or v |
| Γ (γ) | Gamma | g |
| Δ (δ) | Delta | d |
| E (ε) | Epsilon | e |
| Z (ζ) | Zeta | z |
| H (η) | Eta | e or h |
| Θ (θ) | Theta | th |
| I (ι) | Iota | i or j |
| K (κ) | Kappa | c, k, or q |
| Λ (λ) | Lambda | l |
| M (μ) | Mu | m |
| N (ν) | Nu | n |
| Ξ (ξ) | Xi | x |
| O (o) | Omicron | short o |
| Π (π) | Pi | p |
| P (ρ) | Rho | r |
| Σ (σ,ς) | Sigma | s |
| T (τ) | Tau | t |
| Υ (υ) | Upsilon | u or y |
| Φ (φ) | Phi | ph or f |
| X (χ) | Chi | ch |
| Ψ (ψ) | Psi | ps |
| Ω (ω) | Omega | long o |

## GREEK ALPHABET

OUR ALPHABET IS BASED ON THE ONE ANCIENT ROMANS USED. THE ROMANS TOOK THEIR ALPHABET FROM THE ANCIENT GREEKS. THE ANCIENT GREEKS CREDIT HERMES WITH INVENTING THE ALPHABET. SOME OF THE LETTERS ARE VERY SIMILAR TO THE ONES WE USE TODAY.

Hermes used his intelligence and talents for so much more. He is credited with numerous inventions that helped mankind. The ancient Greeks believe Hermes made up numbers and musical instruments. He also worked with the Fates to create the Greek alphabet. Hermes was worshiped throughout Greece as the god of literature, public speaking, and as a patron of poetry. Yet he was known for much more than language and writing.

Hermes was the patron god of athletes as well. He was an athletic young god like his brother Apollo. The ancient Greeks believed he invented boxing, wrestling, footraces, and gymnastics. Despite this, Apollo beat Hermes in a footrace at the very first Olympic games. Gymnasiums contained statues of Hermes and bore his name. Many festivals and athletic contests known as Hermoea were held in honor of Hermes. Hermes was a god with multiple talents who made many contributions to man.

One other important job was given to Hermes. He was the conductor of the dead. Hermes' role was to escort the souls of the dead to the underworld. He traveled with them as far as the river Styx. Once at the river, Hermes turned the souls over to Charon. He was the ferryman for Hades, the god of the underworld. Charon took the souls down the river to the underworld.

There were many sides to Hermes, both good and bad. He was a popular subject of storytellers in ancient times. Audiences were always entertained by his pranks.

Hermes is best known for being the messenger of the gods. After his problem with Apollo had been solved, Hermes still needed to be punished. Hermes managed to charm his father. Zeus promised to make Hermes his messenger, but Hermes could never tell another lie. Then Zeus gave him the gifts he would need for the job. First came a pair of winged sandals called *talaria*. These allowed Hermes to travel at the speed of wind. Next came a cape and a wide-brimmed hat called a *petasus*. Finally Hermes traded his reed pipes to Apollo for the *caduceus*, or messenger staff. Now Hermes was ready to undertake missions on behalf of the gods.

Hermes became the personal messenger of Zeus. The Olympic gods knew Hermes was a trickster, but they trusted him. His slyness and intelligence meant that most of Hermes's missions were successful. Hermes helped Zeus in his battle against the Typhon, a monster created by Gaea to fight Zeus. He helped Ares, the god of war, escape from the Aloadae giants. Hermes even hid Dionysus, the god of wine, at birth from the wrath of Hera.

## CADUCEUS

HERMES'S STAFF WAS CALLED A CADUCEUS. ORIGINALLY IT WAS MADE OF OLIVE BRANCHES. IT HAD TWO SNAKES TWISTED AROUND IT. SOMETIMES IT IS SHOWN WITH WINGS

TO REPRESENT HERMES'S SPEED. ROMAN MESSENGERS USED A STAFF TO IDENTIFY
THEM AS MESSENGERS. IT ALLOWED THEM TO TRAVEL FREELY. THE CADUCEUS WAS
A SYMBOL OF PEACE TO THE ANCIENT GREEKS AND ROMANS. IT WAS THE BADGE
OF MESSENGERS. TODAY IT IS OFTEN USED AS A SYMBOL OF MEDICINE.

One of Hermes's most well known adventures involved his father. Zeus had fallen in love with a woman named Io. Hera learned of the affair and was furious. Zeus was forced to change Io into a white cow to protect her from Hera. Zeus claimed the cow was a gift for Hera. But Hera was not fooled. She placed the cow in her garden and set her guard Argus to watch it. Argus was a giant with 100 eyes.

Zeus asked Hermes for help. Hermes was clever and came up with a plan to free Io. Hermes disguised himself as a shepherd. Argus was excited to have a visitor. First Hermes played Argus some music. Then he began to tell Argus a tale. It was a long and boring story that had no beginning or end. It was so boring it made Argus sleepy. He closed 50 of his eyes. Then he closed the other 50 eyes. Hermes then killed the monster.

## ISIS

HERA ALSO TORMENTED IO BY SENDING A GADFLY AFTER HER. IT CHASED THE COW ALL THE WAY TO EGYPT. WHEN THE ANCIENT EGYPTIANS BEHELD THE WHITE COW, THEY WORSHIPED IT. HERA EVENTUALLY STOPPED BOTHERING IO. SHE ALLOWED ZEUS TO RETURN IO TO HUMAN FORM. IO LATER MARRIED AND BORE A SON WHO BECAME THE KING OF EGYPT. SHE RESEMBLED ISIS, THE ANCIENT EGYPTIAN GODDESS OF FERTILITY, AND WAS SOMETIMES CALLED BY HER NAME.

Another adventure involved the Greek hero Perseus. He had been sent on a mission to collect the head of Medusa—a hideous snake-haired monster. She could turn men to stone with just her gaze. Zeus asked his children Athena, the goddess of war, and Hermes to help Perseus succeed.

The two gods agreed and met Perseus. Athena lent Perseus her shield. Its surface was as shiny as a mirror. Hermes gave Perseus his sword. It was sharp enough to cut through the toughest metal. Athena and Hermes knew the way to the island where Medusa lived, but Perseus needed more tools to succeed. So Hermes flew Perseus to see the Graeae. They were the only ones with directions to the nymphs of the north. The nymphs had the final magical items Perseus needed to beat Medusa. Perseus tricked the Graeae into giving him the information he needed.

Perseus went to the nymphs and collected the final items—a cap of invisibility and a magical bag. The nymphs then pointed Perseus in the direction of the island where Medusa lived. Perseus succeeded in his quest.

## THE GRAEAE

THE GRAEAE WERE THREE OLD WOMEN KNOWN AS THE GRAY SISTERS. THE SISTERS GOT THEIR NAME FROM HAVING GRAY HAIR SINCE BIRTH. DAUGHTERS OF THE TITANS PHORCYS AND CETO, THE GRAEAE WERE GUARDIANS OF MEDUSA

AND HER SISTERS. THE GRAY SISTERS' NAMES WERE ENYO (MEANING HORROR),
DEINO (MEANING DREAD), AND PEMPHREDO (MEANING ALARM). THEY HAD ONLY
ONE EYE AND ONE TOOTH BETWEEN THE THREE OF THEM THAT THEY SHARED.

Hermes was popular with both humans and gods alike. While Hermes had many loves, he never married. His did have several children, however. One of his sons was the god of nature, Pan.

Pan's mother was a wood nymph. She thought Pan looked so strange at birth that she ran off in fright. Pan had the legs of a goat, pointed ears, and small horns. His body was covered in dark shaggy fur. Hermes loved his funny-looking boy. He brought Pan with him to Mount Olympus to amuse the other gods. Pan quickly won their hearts. When Pan returned to Earth, the gods placed him in charge of nature. His home became the dark woods and stony hills of Greece.

Pan was a moody and noisy god. Musical like his father Hermes, Pan also invented an instrument. He created the panpipes and played them as he chased nymphs through the woods.

## AUTOLYCUS

AUTOLYCUS WAS ANOTHER SON OF THE GOD HERMES. HIS MOTHER WAS THE BEAUTIFUL NYMPH CHIONE. AUTOLYCUS HAD HIS FATHER'S SKILLS FOR TRICKERY. AUTOLYCUS POSSESSED THE ABILITY TO CHANGE THE SHAPE OF ANYTHING HE STOLE. HE COULD THEN MAKE IT AND HIMSELF INVISIBLE. AUTOLYCUS BECAME ONE OF THE MOST FAMOUS THIEVES IN ALL OF ANCIENT GREECE.

Hermes appeared in more myths and stories than any other god, though he was often only a supporting character. Hermes was a favorite of storytellers and audiences. His mischief and trickery made for very entertaining stories.

Hermes was the protector of travelers. To help travelers, Hermes liked to remove stones from roads to keep travelers safe. Stones were collected in piles around roadside pillars. Over time these piles became more elaborate. They were dedicated as shrines to honor Hermes. The name *Hermes* comes from the Greek word *herma*, which means "pile of marker stones."

A god of many talents and gifts, Hermes brought a sense of humor to Mount Olympus. He was able to perform all his godly duties, but he was able to have fun, too. It is no wonder Hermes remains a favorite in Greek mythology today.

## THE ROMAN GOD MERCURY

THE ROMAN GOD MERCURY RESEMBLED THE GOD HERMES. AS A RESULT THE ANCIENT ROMANS ADOPTED MANY OF HERMES'S MYTHS. MERCURY WAS WORSHIPED AS THE GOD OF COMMERCE, PROPERTY, AND WEALTH. HIS NAME CAN BE FOUND IN THE WORDS *MERCHANDISE, MERCHANT,* AND *COMMERCE.* MERCURY HAD A TEMPLE IN ROME THAT WAS DEDICATED IN 495 BC. THE TEMPLE WAS LOCATED NEAR THE CIRCUS MAXIMUS, A RACETRACK. IT WAS A GOOD FIT FOR THE GOD OF PROFIT AND TRADE.

# PRINCIPAL GODS OF GREEK MYTHOLOGY – A FAMILY TREE

EROS

ARES    HEBE    HEPHAESTUS    ATHENA    PERSEPHONE    APOLLO    ARTEMIS    HERMES    APHRODITE

ZEUS — MAIA     ZEUS — DIONE

POSEIDON   HADES   HESTIA   HERA   ZEUS   DEMETER     ATLAS   PROMETHEUS   EPIMETHEUS

CRONUS     RHEA     COEUS   PHOEBE     OCEANUS — TETHYS

LETO — ZEUS

IAPETUS

GAEA
*(Earth)*     URANUS
*(Heaven)*

# THE ROMAN GODS

As the Roman Empire expanded by conquering new lands the Romans often took on aspects of the customs and beliefs of the people they conquered. From the ancient Greeks they took their arts and sciences. They also adopted many of their gods and the myths that went with them into their religious beliefs. While the names were changed, the stories and legends found a new home.

**ZEUS:** *Jupiter*
*King of the Gods, God of Sky and Storms*
Symbols: *Eagle and Thunderbolt*

**HERA:** *Juno*
*Queen of the Gods, Goddess of Marriage*
Symbols: *Peacock, Cow, and Crow*

**POSEIDON:** *Neptune*
*God of the Sea and Earthquakes*
Symbols: *Trident, Horse, and Dolphin*

**HADES:** *Pluto*
*God of the Underworld*
Symbols: *Helmet, Metals, and Jewels*

**ATHENA:** *Minerva*
*Goddess of Wisdom, War, and Crafts*
Symbols: *Owl, Shield, and Olive Branch*

**ARES:** *Mars*
*God of War*
Symbols: *Vulture and Dog*

**ARTEMIS:** *Diana*
*Goddess of Hunting and Protector of Animals*
Symbols: *Stag and Moon*

**APOLLO:** *Apollo*
*God of the Sun, Healing, Music, and Poetry*
Symbols: *Laurel, Lyre, Bow, and Raven*

**HEPHAESTUS:** *Vulcan*
*God of Fire, Metalwork, and Building*
Symbols: *Fire, Hammer, and Donkey*

**APHRODITE:** *Venus*
*Goddess of Love and Beauty*
Symbols: *Dove, Sparrow, Swan, and Myrtle*

**EROS:** *Cupid*
*God of Love*
Symbols: *Quiver and Arrows*

**HERMES:** *Mercury*
*God of Travels and Trade*
Symbols: *Staff, Winged Sandals, and Helmet*

# FURTHER INFORMATION

## BOOKS

Green, Jen. *Ancient Greek Myths*. New York: Gareth Stevens, 2010.

Napoli, Donna Jo. *Treasury of Greek Mythology: Classic Stories of Gods, Goddesses, Heroes & Monsters*. Washington, DC: National Geographic Society, 2011.

Reusser, Kayleen. *Hermes*. Hockessin, DE: Mitchell Lane, 2010.

## WEB SITES

Visit our Web site for links about Hermes:
**childsworld.com/links**

*Note to Parents, Teachers, and Librarians: We routinely verify our Web links to make sure they are safe and active sites. So encourage your readers to check them out!*

# INDEX

MAR -- 2013